Ned
and the
Joybaloo

text by
Hiawyn Oram
pictures by
Satoshi Kitamura

Farrar Straus Giroux
New York

SONG OF THE WIND

Every day of the week except Friday, Ned woke up with a frown on his face and some gruff words for a mother who seemed to expect him to wash, dress, have breakfast, and get to school all in the same minute.

But on Fridays he woke up with a smile as bright as an upside-down rainbow.

Friday was the day of the night he met the Joybaloo.

Not that meeting a Joybaloo had been easy for Ned.

He'd looked in everything, under everything, through everything, behind everything. He'd even looked in places he knew a Joybaloo could not possibly be.

Then one Friday night he'd gone to the
linen closet in search of an important
piece of a thing he was making and there it
was, when he wasn't expecting it, big and
beautiful, with a funny leathery nose and its
breath full of paper roses.

Together he and the Joybaloo danced across the landing and onto Ned's bed.

They bounced high and they bounced higher, till the ceiling opened and let in the stars.

They made each other laugh so much their laughter propelled them up, up, and on past every-day night and every-night dreams to the playgrounds of the Joybaloo.

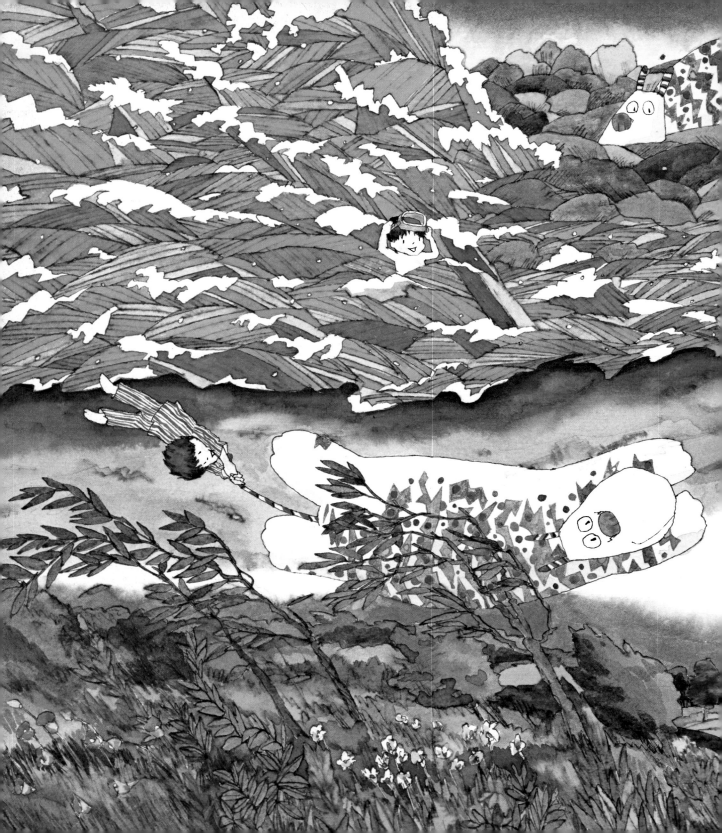

There they slid in the slow dark mud and swam in the warm fast streams. They ran wild with the wind and lost themselves for hours in the long wayward grass.

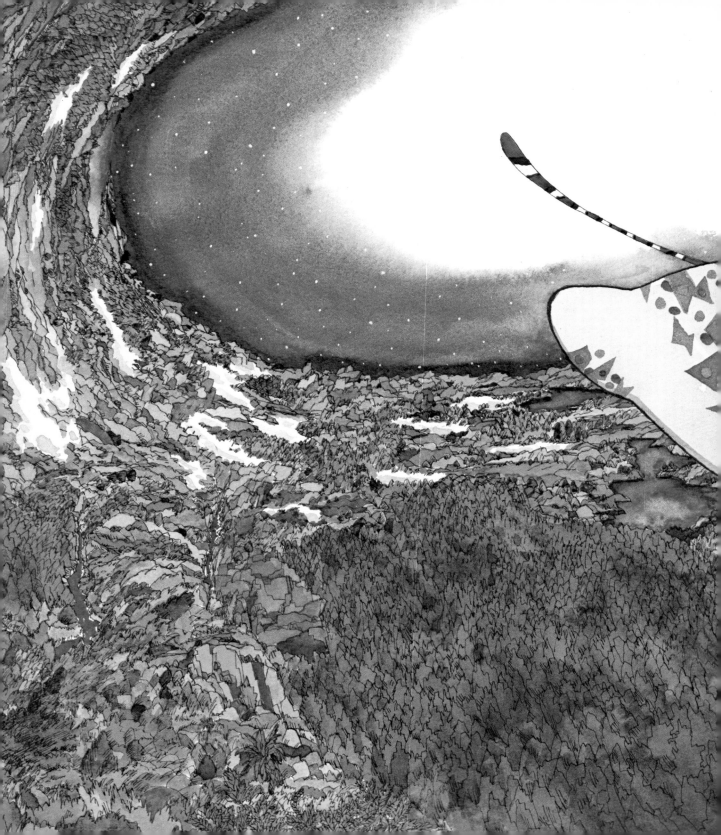

When they'd squeezed the last drop of mischief out of the night, they promised to meet at the same time in the same place the next Friday and every Friday forever.

So how did next Friday begin to seem like never?
Ned didn't know, but it did. He began to want more.
He began to want lots. He began to want every night to
be Joybaloo night.

To fill in the time between one Friday and the next, he became impossible.

He wouldn't eat. He wouldn't practice his recorder. He drew on every wall and put tacks in people's shoes.

He stayed awake deep into the night when he might have been sleeping and growing.

"I don't believe you're a real Joybaloo. You don't even breathe real roses. If you were and you cared about me, you'd come out to play every night."

"Can't," said the Joybaloo, "or I get used up."

But Ned was not listening.

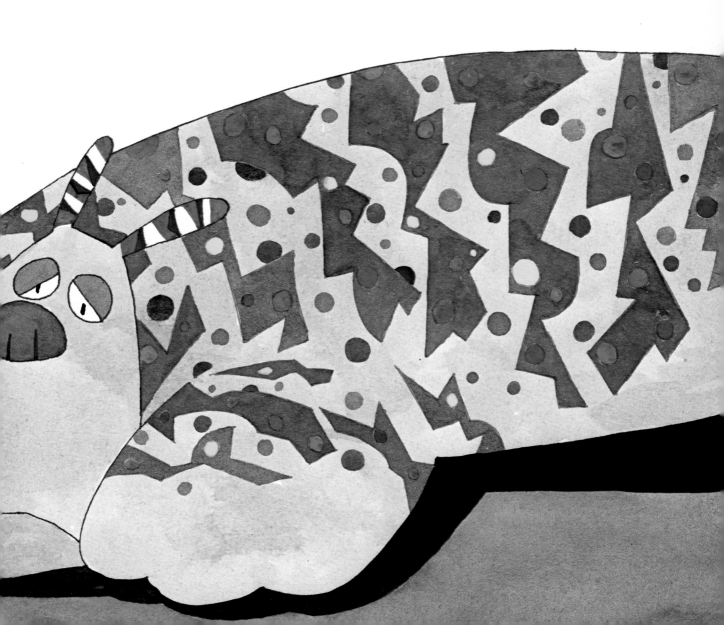

He pushed and pulled until he got his way.
He didn't seem to notice that each time the
Joybaloo came out when it wanted to sleep, their
bouncing got a little lower and their laughter a
little less.

He didn't seem to notice the Joybaloo getting smaller and smaller, its colors fewer and fewer, its breath emptier and emptier, until one night when he opened the linen-closet door

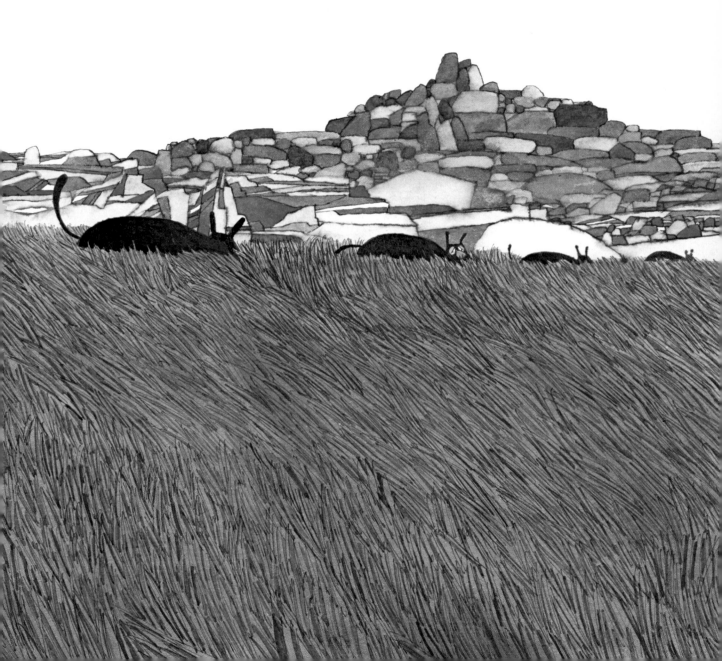

THERE WAS NOTHING THERE.

After that, Ned had no choice but to start making his own joy.

To his surprise, he found it wasn't so hard.

Once he even picked his HURRY-UP-I-WARN-YOU
mother a bunch of flowers so he could enjoy watching
her trying not to smile.

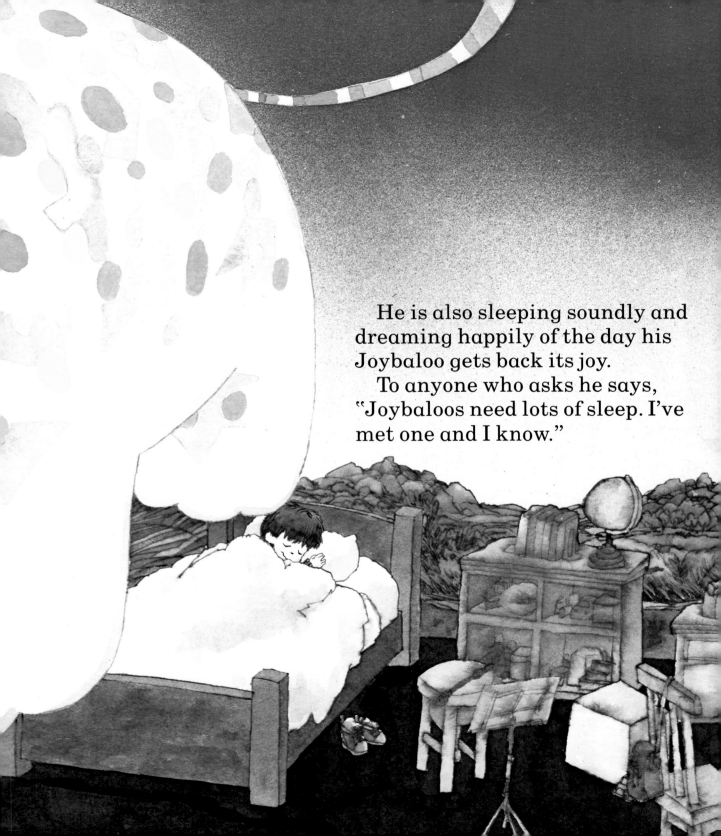

He is also sleeping soundly and
dreaming happily of the day his
Joybaloo gets back its joy.
To anyone who asks he says,
"Joybaloos need lots of sleep. I've
met one and I know."